Poetry For Performance

An Anthology for Speech and Drama Teachers

Also by The Playing Space

Acting Exams: A Teacher's Guide
Scenes From The Classics: The Jungle Book

The Playing Space

Poetry For Performance

An Anthology for Speech and Drama Teachers

VOLUME 1

First published in Great Britain in 2017
by
The Playing Space,
5 Bridge Road,
London N22 7SN,
United Kingdom

ISBN 978-1-5464-2191-7

Poetry For Performance: An Anthology for Speech and Drama Teachers
Copyright © The Playing Space 2017

The Playing Space is hereby identified as author of this compilation in accordance with the Copyright, Designs and Patents Act, 1988. The contributors are hereby identified as authors of their contributions.

All rights reserved. No part of this publication may be reproduced, stored in a retrieval system or transmitted in any form or by any means, electronic, mechanical, photocopying, recording or otherwise without the prior written permission of the publisher and copyright owner.

theplayingspace.co.uk/books/
books@theplayingspace.co.uk

Cover photograph © Ian Francis

A NOTE FOR TEACHERS

We have chosen the poems in this book because we feel they are particularly suitable for performing aloud. They are brand new poems that you won't find in any other anthology and are therefore an excellent choice for speech and drama exams and for drama festivals.

We have arranged the poems under the following headings:

AGES 6 – 10: These poems are suitable for exams at Entry Level and at Grades 1 and 2.
AGES 10 – 14: These poems are suitable for exams at Grades 3 – 5.
AGES 14+: These poems are suitable for exams at Grade 6 and above.
SONNETS: These poems are perfect for LAMDA Grade 7 Verse and Prose exams.

Broadly speaking, the poems within each age range become more complex as you move through. They might increase in difficulty because of length, vocabulary and concepts.

CONTENTS

How to Become Brilliant at Performing Poetry   1

Poems For Ages 6–10

Crabs *by Harris Goldberg*	6
Cats *by Zöe Street*	7
In The Rain *by Alison Chisholm*	9
Zebra *by Sheila Stevens*	10
The Giant *by Emma Wolfe*	11
Witches *by Emma Wolfe*	12
On The Bridge *by Margaret Whyte*	13
Twirling *by Ros Woolner*	14
My Favourite Colour *by Gabi Maddocks*	15
FIFA 17 *by Ros Woolner*	16
Louisa And The Field Mouse *by Amy Buxton*	17
Barnabas And Me *by Sylvia Lees*	19
Tangled Laces *by Gabi Maddocks*	21
How To Terrify A Mole *by Emma Wolfe*	23
Byron Tries To Knit *by Alison Chisholm*	24
Spider In The Classroom *by Anita Loughrey*	26
Maybe One Day *by Gabi Maddocks*	28
Harvest Supper *by Susan Rogerson*	29
Aliens Under The Bed *by Shirley Tomlinson*	30
A Very Scary Teacher *by Shirley Tomlinson*	32

Poems For Ages 10–14

Maximilian's Whale *by Sheila Stevens*	34
Uncle Bernie's Beard *by Karen Pailing*	36
Natural Autumn *by Peter Dean*	38
There's Nothing Under The Bed *by Alex Woolf*	40
Looking Out *by Karen Pailing*	42
Odd Footprints On An Empty Beach *by Sylvia Lees*	44
Late *by Gabi Maddocks*	45
Dear Father Christmas *by Susan Rogerson*	47
What Lies Beyond *by Gabi Maddocks*	49
Snake Meets Man *by Emma Wolfe*	51
Dead Bird Talking *by Anne Harding*	52
The Fairground *by Anita Loughrey*	54
The Country Squire *by Susan Rogerson*	56
Natterjack *by Karen Pailing*	58
Trout In A Top Hat *by Susan Rogerson*	59
Surfing Spider *by Karen Pailing*	61
Little Brother *by Ros Woolner*	63
Mere Words *by Kelly Davis*	65

Poems for Ages 14 and Above

Beachcombing *by Alison Chisholm*	67
The Short View *by Ali Pickford*	69
Gooseberries *by Lynne Sutton*	72
One Day *by Emma-Louise Tinniswood*	75
A Hurried Confession *by Freya Carroll*	77
Priceless *by Freya Carroll*	81
Hearing The Echoes *by Kelly Davis*	83
Seagull's Swooping Attack *by Kelly Davis*	86
Tribal Voices *by Kelly Davis*	88
Mr Falstaff *by David Maddison*	90
Floating *by Susan Rogerson*	92
Out, Damned Spot *by Susan Rogerson*	94
Please Will Someone Feed The Cat? *by Susan Rogerson*	97
Recapturing The Magic *by Susan Rogerson*	100
Suffocation *by Susan Rogerson*	103
The Lollipop Tree *by Susan Rogerson*	106
Crash *by Amy Shearer*	109
Pink Eye/Stink Eye In San Francisco *by Amy Shearer*	111
Maureen, In Her Chair *by Kelly Davis*	116
Life In The Old Dog *by Kelly Davis*	119

Sonnets

Mermaid *by Susan Rogerson* — 121

When Forty Years Have Passed
by Kelly Davis — 122

The Spider And The Fly *by Susan Rogerson* — 123

Embers *by Kelly Davis* — 124

Jessica *by Kelly Davis* — 125

Serpent's Tongue *by Susan Rogerson* — 126

Who Can Know *by Susan Cartwright-Smith* — 127

The Bottom Of The Jar
by Susan Cartwright-Smith — 128

Acknowledgements — 129
Index of Poets — 131
Index of Titles — 132

HOW TO BECOME BRILIANT AT PERFORMING POETRY

1. Memory
It's always a good idea to learn your poem off by heart – unless there is a specific reason not to (in a LAMDA Reading For Performance exam, for example, you must read from a printed text). Some fortunate people learn lines very quickly, but for most, it takes time and effort. Learn your poem one line at a time, rather than trying to learn the whole thing at once. Record yourself saying your poem aloud from memory. Then listen back, following the text, and look out for mistakes. Punctuation is very important and also needs to be learned.

2. Posture
Your job is to share the meaning of the poem with the audience. Too much movement and action can be distracting, so stand still while you say your poem, with your feet slightly apart so that you don't wobble and your hands loosely by your sides. Some spontaneous gesture or movement is fine, but expression should come primarily from the face and the voice. It is a good

idea to practice in front of a mirror so you can check that you're not wriggling and fidgeting.

3. Pace

Most people performing poetry for the first time have a tendency to rush. Some even treat verse speaking as a race and think that the quicker they get to the end of the poem, the better. In fact the opposite is true. Your audience needs time to listen to and enjoy the poem. If you time an experienced performer saying the poem, you will have an idea of how long it should take. Then you can practise slowing down so that you take the same amount of time to read the poem. If you have a habit of going too fast, remember that in order to get to the right speed, the poem should sound strangely slow to you – until you get used to the correct pace.

Variety is also important. If you get stuck on the same speed, whether fast or slow, your audience is likely to lose interest. A fast pace could signify excitement or fear, whereas a slower pace could indicate a dreamy mood or could be used to draw the audience into a secret. Look through your poem and find places where you can pick up the pace and others where you can slow down.

4. Pause

Pause after the introduction, whenever there is punctuation and between stanzas. You should also pause right at the end, before you come out of 'performance mode'. Work out how many pauses there should be and then ask someone else to listen to you and count the number of pauses they heard – did you include them all? Remember that taking a pause does not mean you stop performing. The pause is where you allow the audience (and yourself) a moment to absorb the words and ideas.

5. Audibility

You don't need to shout, even if you are performing in a large hall. However, you do want your audience to hear you. You need to use a strong voice and you need to speak clearly. Imagine that your voice flows from your mouth like paint. Try to cover every wall and the floor and ceiling of the room. Can you 'paint' every corner of the space with your voice? Practise at home with someone standing in another room, or at the end of a corridor, or the top of the stairs. Can they still hear every word? If you are rehearsing your poem in a small space, then imagine that your audience is on the other side of the wall, or out in the garden. Doing so will help you get used to the louder sound and the feeling of a stronger voice until it feels quite natural.

6. Clarity

If you speak clearly, so that every consonant sound is crisp and punchy, then it is much easier for your audience to follow every word that you are saying. The best way to improve your clarity is to practice tongue-twisters every day. Say a tongue-twister slowly a few times. If you manage to say it clearly without making a mistake, speed up. There are lots of popular tongue-twisters, but here are a few of my favourites:

> *Red lorry, yellow lorry, red lorry, yellow lorry* (repeat ten times).
> *You know unique New York? New York's unique, you know.*
> *There's a chip shop in space that sells spaceship-shaped chips.*
> *What time does the wrist-watch strap shop shut?*
> *Theo the thistle-sifter thrust his two thumbs through the thick thistles.*

If you can say those, you can say anything!

7. Expression

Your ultimate goal is to share your poem with expression. Go through the poem and identify the different feelings in it. There will usually be more than one option, so there is no 'right answer'. Pick two or three emotions that fit the meaning of the poem, and then try them out. Is there one that feels better than the others? Keep experimenting. The important thing is to make a choice and then to be brave and commit to that choice. You need to show the feelings with your face, your eyes and your voice. Ask a friend to watch you practice and see if they can guess the emotions – if they guess correctly then you know you are on the right track. The following emotion words should give you some initial ideas:

Aggressive	Confused	Frightened	Peaceful
Amazed	Contemptuous	Hopeful	Petrified
Amused	Despairing	Jealous	Proud
Angry	Disgusted	Kindhearted	Relaxed
Ashamed	Distracted	Loving	Shocked
Brave	Embarrassed	Miserable	Stressed
Cautious	Excited	Nervous	Surprised
Confident	Exhausted	Passionate	Worried

CRABS

Harris Goldberg

A lonely crab crawled on the shore,
The tide came in and now there's more.
The tide came in and washed them all
And now there's ninety-four.
They're orange and red with claws that shine,
They wriggle and wave them in the brine.
In the bay the rocks are grey,
The sun shines in the sky.
People swim and splash around
And say 'Bye, crabs, bye-bye!'

CATS
Zöe Street

Cats.

They're fussy eaters

Love their heaters

Sleepy eyes

Hypnotise

Comfy beds

For sleepy heads

Fluffy toys

Rolling balls

Emerald eyes

Like little jewels

Delicate whiskers

Tiny paws

That cover up their needle claws!

Playful mood

Squeaky mouse

Chase it, chase it round the house

Washing time

Lick lick lick

continued ▶

POETRY FOR PERFORMANCE

◀ *CATS by Zöe Street*

Tired now
Curl up small
In a ball
And sleep.

6 – 10 YEARS

IN THE RAIN
Alison Chisholm

We're playing football in the rain,
but I don't care – I love the game.

My Mum will not be very pleased –
there's mud all over both my knees.

Mud's in my eyes and up my nose,
mud's oozing out between my toes.

Mud's up my arms and in my hair
and down my shorts and everywhere;

And when Mum sees my yellow shirt
she'll scream with rage at all that dirt.

But I don't mind – I'll take the blame –
'cause football's still my favourite game.

ZEBRA

Sheila Stevens

When I was three and nearly four
I had two pets but wanted more.
'A zebra, please', I asked, 'with stripes'.
'A what?' laughed Dad. My brother said 'Cripes!'
Mum said, 'Zebras must live in a zoo.
Wouldn't you like a cockatoo?
Now please don't start to cry, my dear.
A zebra wouldn't be happy here'.

I begged until my birthday came,
But everyone just said the same.
'You can't have a zebra and that is that!'
So, instead I got a stripey cat.

I called her Zebra.

THE GIANT
Emma Wolfe

Playing down by the old sea-shore,
Where the angry giant roars,
Listen to the giant growl
Hear his foot falls thudding down.

Feel the shudder – it runs through
Your bones as he approaches you.
Don't listen to the squelch and crunch
As you become the Giant's lunch.

WITCHES
Emma Wolfe

Witches gather round log fires
For seeing flaming sticks inspires
Them to think up gruesome potions,
Fearsome magic, spells and lotions.

In groups they huddle, emitting wails,
Rubbing their hands with inch-long nails
While their brains work like machines
To think of ways to make men scream.

ON THE BRIDGE

Margaret Whyte

The river comes. The river goes.
Hey Ho the little fishes.
I feed them sweets from off the bridge,
And pray they'll grant my wishes.

I wish for sunflowers round my bed.
I wish for sunshine in my head.
I wish a pirate from the sea,
Would want to come and marry me.

The river comes. The river goes.
Hey Ho the little fishes.
They swim on both sides of the bridge.
Hey Ho what chance my wishes?

TWIRLING
Ros Woolner

I am a little girl
who loves to spin and twirl
and climb and skip and hop –
I simply cannot stop.
I glide from door to door,
socks polishing the floor,
climb over backs of chairs
and slide feet-first downstairs.
'Why won't she walk?' they say.
'Why spin and slide all day?'
'Why jump and climb around?'
'Why not stay on the ground?'
Most grownups do not know
why twirling thrills me so.
You want to know the answer?
I'm going to be a dancer!

MY FAVOURITE COLOUR
Gabi Maddocks

White is clean sheets on my newly made bed.
A bowl full of strawberries: that is Red.
Green is the grass beneath my feet
Covered in dew, transparent and sweet.
Yellow is sunshine that warms my skin.
Blue is the water I'm splashing in.
Crumbling soil: that is Brown,
Cream is an egg or fluffy goose down.
Black is shadows, a forest at night,
Beneath my bed, no sound, no sight.
Which is my favourite? Which is the best?
Which one do I like so much more than the rest?
I choose them all, mixed together up high.
Colours merged in a rainbow: The Queen of the Sky.

FIFA 17
Ros Woolner

Heavy-breathing concentration,
thumbs controlling play:
Wolves are beating Albion
7–5 away.
Sliding tackle on the wing,
Wolves have lost possession.
West Brom strikers pass and score
three times in succession.
Two minutes left of normal time,
the Wanderers equalize.
Can they win this after all
and carry home the prize?
Edwards passes to Dicko.
'Go on, score!' But then…
'Switch it off now,' Mum insists,
'It's nearly half past ten.'

LOUISA AND THE FIELD MOUSE
Amy Buxton

Louisa was walking through a field of long grass,
When she stopped for a moment
To let a mouse pass.
The mouse turned and said:
'Madame, why did you pause?'
'To let you pass, my dear friend,'
And she shook his two paws.
'I'm not often noticed –
I'm incredibly small.'
'Small you may be,
But you're bold as the tall,
As brave as a giant
But friendlier too,
And I think we'll be friends,
Good ones, and true.'
'Well, what are you up to?
I could show you around.
The field's more exciting
When you're close to the ground.'
Louisa agreed, but she asked the dear mouse
If later he'd visit her own little house.

continued ▶

POETRY FOR PERFORMANCE

◀ *LOUISA AND THE FIELD MOUSE by Amy Buxton*

'You can sit on my shoulder and I'll show you around,
Though it's a bit colder when you're high off the
    ground.'
They nodded together,
And held on to each other
And saw their own world through the eyes of another.

6 – 10 YEARS

BARNABAS AND ME
Sylvia Lees

I have a baby brother
His name is Barnabas
When people see him in his pram
They always make a fuss.

They use a funny language
Mum calls it baby talk
And they use it when they notice
We're going for a walk.

Grandma scented in her frock
Grips Barney's pram and makes it rock
'Who's my sweetie darling boy?
Goo-gah goo-gah goo-gah GOY!'

Brother Tim puts his head in
With grubby face and sticky chin
Tries to share his chocolate ice
'Lick-a lick-a Barney – nice!'

continued ▶

POETRY FOR PERFORMANCE

◀ *BARNABAS AND ME by Sylvia Lees*

Our neighbour spots Barney's pram
'Oh what a bonny bonny lamb!
Like his Mum and like his Dad
Gaddy gaddy gaddy GAD!'

I really wish they would suss
That Barnabas gets all the fuss
I really wish they would see
Wish they'd save some fuss for me!

TANGLED LACES
Gabi Maddocks

My running shoes help me win races,
But the problem comes with the laces:
They loosen, you see,
So I fall on my knee
And get grazes in all sorts of places!

If I only had Velcro straps
I could run laps and laps
I could leap over ditches
Without any hitches
And never get into mishaps.

My mum ties my laces 'just so'
In a perfect rabbit-ear bow
But they don't stay that way
Not for the whole day
And I end up head-over-toe.

continued ▶

POETRY FOR PERFORMANCE

◀ *TANGLED LACES by Gabi Maddocks*

But now there's no need to be glum:
I've padded my knees up with gum!
So now when I fall
It won't hurt at all
They just feel a little bit numb.

HOW TO TERRIFY A MOLE
Emma Wolfe

There was a rabbit in a hole.
Her next door neighbour was a mole.
They met one day for a cup of tea
And mole said 'Will you marry me?'
The delighted rabbit danced with glee
And shouted to the rooftops 'YES!'
And ran to the shops to buy a dress
A great big smile on her face.
(The dress she chose was covered in lace
With sequins twinkling all over the place.)

Then she went to book the hall
Where they'd have their wedding ball.
She bought a cake, confetti too,
Rings and a veil and something blue,
Everything had to be brand new.
Finally she'd found her man
And everything was going to plan.
Except that later on that day
She found the wedding bills to pay
And she'd scared the poor old mole away.

BYRON TRIES TO KNIT
Alison Chisholm

With one slight, careless flick
of a marmalade paw,
he brushes my ball of wool
onto the floor,
where it rolls to provoke him.
He quivers, then leaps,
and scatters my patterns
from nice tidy heaps
to a chaos of paper.
He charges and dives –
then with claws just as sharp
as the sharpest of knives
he teases the wool
and he pulls it in knots
and unravels the strands.
Then he ponders and plots
how to add to the game –
bats the wool round a chair,
beneath the TV,
through your legs, up the stair
then back down. Now the yarn

6–10 YEARS

is all tousled and grey
and the only thing left
is to throw it away.
But Byron is purring –
he climbs in my lap
contented, forgiven;
curls up for a nap.

SPIDER IN THE CLASSROOM
Anita Loughrey

There's a spider in the classroom
Under Miss Blake's chair.
It's big and fat and hairy
And she doesn't know it's there.

I watch it roam the carpet
And imagine what she'll do.
I wonder, should I tell her
It's crawling around her shoe?

Miss Blake continues the story,
The spider continues to crawl.
It slowly creeps up the chair leg
Miss Blake hasn't noticed at all.

The eight hairy legs wiggle wildly
As it sneaks into the folds of her dress.
Miss Blake's still reading the story,
The spider climbs up to her chest.

6 – 10 YEARS

She screams,
She shouts,
We leap about.
The spider shoots through the air.

There's a spider in the classroom,
Miss Blake is stood upon her chair.
We don't know where it has gone
But everyone knows it's there.

MAYBE ONE DAY
Gabi Maddocks

Why is she looking at me?
I don't have my hand up.
Why is she looking at me?
I don't know the answer.
Why is she looking at me?
I wish I wasn't here.

When she's not looking at me,
I look at her.
Her hair is… fluffy like a nest.
Her eyes are… twinkly like magic.
Her nose is… turned up like a spoilt princess.
Her body is… soft like a cushion.
You can imagine it wrapped round you like a duvet.
She is kind, and her kindness shines out of her.

But when she looks at me
I look away.
Eyes down to my desk.

Maybe one day I'll look back, and smile.

HARVEST SUPPER

Susan Rogerson

Soft silhouette glides across the moon,
merges into sleeping oak.
A banshee screech splits the night –
wood mouse, weaving through grass shadows, jumps –
then freezes, till the startled air is still.

Cautiously she lifts her nose,
drawn by sweet aromas in the hedge,
and there amongst the tangled thorns she finds
the plumpest blackberry.

She nibbles under silver candlelight,
turns it deftly in her tiny paws.
And when her perfect pod of juice is spent,
her sticky nose imbued with purple scent,
she wipes her face in moondrops, then, content,
bounces into the star-soaked night.

ALIENS UNDER THE BED

Shirley Tomlinson

'I just can't go upstairs,' I said,
'there's an alien underneath my bed!'
My mother sighed, 'I'll come up too,
I've really had enough of you
and all the silly lies you tell.
You've made it up. You know quite well.'
She knelt to look. 'Well no one's there…
just smelly socks and underwear,
your trainers, comics and a book,
some grubby shorts… here, take a look.'
'Oh Mum, I bet he's gone to hide.
Open the wardrobe. Look inside.'
She peered inside the wardrobe door…
A PUFF OF SMOKE! A WHIRRING ROAR!
THE WARDROBE SHOT OUT INTO SPACE,
NO MUM! NO ALIEN! NOT A TRACE!

I hope they're back by Saturday,
or what will Mr. Williams say?
A goalie minus football kit!
I really think he'd have a fit.

6 – 10 YEARS

How could I tell him to his face
my football kit's in outer space,
locked in a wardrobe far away?
OH PLEASE COME BACK BY SATURDAY!

A VERY SCARY TEACHER

Shirley Tomlinson

When Mrs. Brown was off with 'flu,
We were taught by Mr. Springer.
He had a dalek sort of voice
And a ring on every finger.

One day when all the class had gone,
I went back for a book.
'What do you want?' Mr. Springer said.
He fixed me with a look.

And then his eyes flashed on and off,
Amber, red and green
Exactly like the traffic lights,
And he looked extremely mean.

I didn't wait to find the book,
But ran out straight away,
Right across the car park
Where we're not supposed to play.

The car park was deserted
Except for Springer's car,
Long and sleek and silver,
And sparkly like a star.

I saw him open up the door
And climb into his seat.
Vroom vroom vroom! He sped away
Zipping down the street.

And as I watched, the car took off!
I swear to you it's true.
Above the trees and house tops…
And into space it flew.

MAXIMILIAN'S WHALE
Sheila Stevens

Maximilian McCorkendale
Has always wanted to see a whale.
Not just in books or on the TV,
But swimming beside him in the sea.

'Dad, when it's time for our holiday,
can we go to Iceland or even Norway,
to see whales swim in the sea?'

'They're just too far away', Dad said.
'Blackpool will be fun instead
and *you* can swim in the sea!'

Max lies on the beach thinking only of whales.
He's tired of sandcastles, spades and pails.
'No, I don't want to swim in the sea!'

A sudden splash makes him sit up and stare.
What's that shape in the water there?
A jet of water shoots up from the sea
A great tail rises, could it actually be?

'Yes, it is,' gasps Max, 'it's a whale RIGHT HERE
swimming along at the end of the pier.'
The whale swims closer and winks its big eye
as its swishing tail splashes and waves 'Goodbye'.

One last blow and a shower of spray,
A surging dive and it swims away.

'Wake up, Maxie, I've brought you ice-cream.'
Max rubs his eyes, 'Was it only a dream?'
No whale is swimming by Blackpool's pier.
Sadly Max sighs, 'Well, maybe next year.'

UNCLE BERNIE'S BEARD
Karen Pailing

There's something funny, something weird,
about my Uncle Bernie's beard.
It's pretty obvious to me
it's not where it's supposed to be.

He's hairless as a billiard ball
on top, you see – no hair at all.
The stuff that should be on his head
is growing on his chin instead.

I'm trying hard to be polite.
I'm on my best behaviour, right?
But still I ask, 'Are you a clown?
Your head's been glued on upside down.'

My sister giggles. Mum goes red
and splutters, 'You'll get sent to bed
if you don't mind your attitude.
You can't say things like that. It's rude.'

They're all embarrassed and confused,
but Uncle Bernie seems amused.
I'm sure that I detect a grin
behind his bushy-whiskered chin.

He leans across and winks. 'It's fine.
It's dropped a bit, but it's all mine.
And, now I'm used to it, I've found
I much prefer it this way round.

For instance, only yesterday,
I glued it on the other way.
And almost everyone agreed
that it looked very strange indeed.'

NATURAL AUTUMN
Peter Dean

Creepy little crawly things,
Under rocks and stones –
Woodlice, spiders, ants and more,
Looking for a home.

Rotting leaves, and little twigs,
Decaying slowly there.
Micro-fauna chomping mad
Beneath the autumn air.

A blackbird pecks, and pecks, and pecks,
In a pile of dusty bricks,
Looking for some tiny grubs
With which to feed her chicks.

Heartened by still warming sun
Before the cold, cold chills,
Mushrooms and other fungi come,
Red caps above their gills.

10 – 14 YEARS

Berries from the hawthorn bush
Glow like secret treasure
Field mice and a flock of birds
Hoard it all with pleasure.

Feeding up, and breaking down,
The cycle never ends.
Days grow shorter, winter waits,
Nature just attends.

THERE'S NOTHING UNDER THE BED
Alex Woolf

There's nothing under the bed at night, when I go to sleep.
There's nothing under the bed at night to make my skin creep,
And if perchance my foot should stray in the region of the floor,
Nothing will reach out and grab me in its scaly claw!

A bump in the night is nothing but the cat jumping onto the chair,
And in such an old house there's nothing odd about a creak upon the stair,
And the crooked shadow at the window that seems to point at me
Is nothing but the branches of an ancient sycamore tree.

There's nothing in the wardrobe, I checked it over twice.
There's nothing in the wardrobe to turn my blood to ice,
And if perchance the door should open, nothing will appear.
No monster, ghoul or demon, to grip my heart with fear.

The shriek of the witch is nothing but the owl in the wood.
The headless monk by the door is only my gown with its hood,
And the eerie smell from beneath my bed of rotting vegetation
Is clearly just the product of my imagination.

There's nothing under the bed at night, when I go to sleep.
There's nothing under the bed at night, to make my skin creep.
So why is it that I have to check, and check again to be sure
That there's nothing down there that can grab me in its scaly claw!

LOOKING OUT
Karen Pailing

I love this goldfish bowl because it's all
I've ever wanted, known or can recall.

It's safe in here, although I have to say
a little claustrophobic. Anyway,

we both know you're in charge. I've never dared
to contemplate escape; I'd be too scared.

I watch you watching afternoon TV
and every now and then you'll smile at me.

But sometimes I feel life has passed me by –
or I've passed life – I can't imagine why.

So, lately, when I'm bored, I'll flip around
and swim the other way; it helps, I've found

to see things from a different point of view:
my world looks quite surreal, and so do you,

10 – 14 YEARS

almost as if I'm on your chintz settee
while you're inside this bowl instead of me.

If only you could do the same, it's clear
to me you'd learn how dull it is in here.

And then – I absolutely guarantee it -
you'd move that telly to where I can see it.

ODD FOOTPRINTS ON AN EMPTY BEACH
Sylvia Lees

What happened on this beach before?
What made those odd prints in the sand?
Are they the marks of man or beast?
Or of some dreadful thing unleashed?

Just who or what arrived or left
Or may still be amongst us now?
My questions mingle with my fear
To spiral-swirl and stab and sear.

The mind is such a fragile thing,
The mind can breed imaginings.
The greatest fear when fear is sown
Is the fear of threat or fate unknown.

But soon the sea will wash away
Those troubling prints which smutch the sand.
There'll be no clouds to mask the sun,
I've faced my fear and peace is won.

LATE
Gabi Maddocks

I came home but he stayed out,
Playing in the park.
What could he be doing
Out there in the dark?

I wish that I could call him
But he doesn't have a phone.
What could he be doing
Out there on his own?

Perhaps I should have waited
But I was getting bored
And wanted to watch the telly
And warm myself indoors.

But now I wish I'd waited
What's taking him so long?
I'm really getting worried,
What if something's wrong?

continued ▶

POETRY FOR PERFORMANCE

◀ *LATE by Gabi Maddocks*

And then there's footsteps on the path
The slamming of the gate
And I hear my voice sound really cross
'Why are you so late?!'

And I hear him mumble, 'Sorry,
The time just seemed to fly.'
And although he sees me grumble
Inside, relieved, I sigh.

DEAR FATHER CHRISTMAS
Susan Rogerson

I know you're really busy in your workshop, making toys
For all the very good and extra-special girls and boys.
I think I must be bad because my daddy's gone away –
I don't think I'll be getting any toys on Christmas Day.
He wasn't there on Sunday when we went to fetch the
   tree,
All the children had their daddy's hand to hold but me.
And Mummy had a struggle when we took it on the bus,
She went a funny red when people stared and laughed
   at us.
My daddy always puts the fairy lights around the tree,
Mummy tried but couldn't get them working properly.
She said it didn't matter if a few lights didn't twinkle,
We'd just put lots of baubles on and add some extra
   tinsel.
But when it came to my job – putting Fairy on the top –
Without my daddy's shoulders, all poor Fairy did was flop.
I think that Mummy misses him, the other day she cried,
She said it was just fairy dust that blew into her eyes.

continued ▶

◀ *DEAR FATHER CHRISTMAS by Susan Rogerson*

She helped me make some Christmas cards with glitter, paint and glue –
I made one just for Daddy, but I said it was for you.
Then Mummy said that you would bring me presents just the same –
But what if Daddy isn't there to play with my new games?
I'll leave you some mince pies that Mummy baked especially,
And carrots for the reindeer – Mummy said they'd help them see.
But I don't want the presents that you bring me in your sack –
PLEASE, Father Christmas, I'll be good – just bring my daddy back.

WHAT LIES BEYOND
Gabi Maddocks

Behind twisting vines of ivy
There's a wall of crumbling brick
That nobody would notice
Through all the leaves so thick.

And there's a door of ancient oak
That somehow seems to glow
It has a lock that's red with rust,
The key lost long ago.

And sometimes when the moon is full
Strange noises reach my ear,
Such ghostly moans and howling
That they fill me up with fear.

And though I'll never find the key
I cannot help but dream
Of what might lie behind the door
Things heard but never seen.

continued ▶

◀ *WHAT LIES BEYOND by Gabi Maddocks*

And when I imagine what might lurk
I'm glad the wall is sound
And I'm glad the key is gone and lost
Never to be found.

SNAKE MEETS MAN
Emma Wolfe

Sliding through the coarse leaves,
Smooth, scaled body weaving through the cotton grass.
Elegant, velvet, soft.
Moving slowly through the sand.

Slanted, peering eyes, alert and aware,
Blue-fringed flickering tongue tasting the hot sun.
Peaceful, relaxed, tired.
A coiled rope in the dunes.

Sudden quick movements in heavy boots,
Quick flick of a net, a spray of sand, a flailing body.
Terrified, angry, confused.
Merry voices fill the air.

Expectant eyes, eagerly watching,
The writhing length, hung by the neck. A knife flashes.
Pain, blood, death.
The loose corpse drops to the ground.

DEAD BIRD TALKING

Anne Harding

I'm a large and cumbersome bird,
With tiny wings, I look absurd,
Unable to fly, my nest on the ground,
Glad no predators were to be found.

I was happy living this way,
Until, that is, one fateful day,
Two legged creatures arrived on the sand,
And decided they liked the look of my land.

To my horror they craved meat,
And so began to kill and eat.
I thought it best to hide in a cave,
Make myself scarce so I'd be saved.

But there was so much worse to come:
Not only did they use a gun
But four legged creatures led the way,
They were trained to search for prey.

They found my nest with eggs in it,
And crushed them all within a minute.
As the last of my kind it was too late
For anyone to prevent my fate.

I'm sure you have guessed my claim to fame
And know that Dodo is my name,
But perhaps you thought I was a myth?
And I need you to know that I really lived.

In museums my bones can be found
To prove that I was once around.
So I am remembered to this day,
As a strange-looking bird, who died away.

THE FAIRGROUND
Anita Loughrey

Laughter and screams
Fairy light beams
Images blur
Flickering stream of light
The Waltzer spins
As colour gyrates
To the mayhem of sound.

Sparks spray
Wires skim the chequered array
Dodgems crash
Carriages thud
Around the circuit
The cars trudge
Past the bedlam of faces.

Generators churning
Slowly turning
The big wheel climbs
To dizzy heights
Snuggling couples

View the sights
A commotion of intertwined places.

Toffee apples crunch
Flocks of children bunch
Flecks of candyfloss
Stuck in their hair
Singing and shouting
Without a care
In the chaos of the fairground.

THE COUNTRY SQUIRE
Susan Rogerson

Who is that dashing country squire,
With breast of burnished copper fire,
Rich russet coat upon his back,
Embroidered threads of pearl and black;
A soft white collar, tucked in which,
A silken turquoise neckerchief,
And on each cheek of his fine-boned head,
A brilliant splash of ruby red?

Who struts on by in grey-stockinged feet,
Along his favoured country beat,
Flicks his coat-tails, puffs his chest,
So the ladies eye him at his best,
And stands aloft his castle mound,
To view his manor lands around,
Alert to any unwise fool,
Who dares engage him in a duel –
Then, rivals vanquished, crowing proudly,
Proclaims his glorious triumphs loudly,

To every being, beast or man,
Throughout his corner of the land?

Who is that master I behold,
That dapper gentleman heretold,
That country squire amid the peasants?

He is, of course, the splendid pheasant!

NATTERJACK
Karen Pailing

We've tried to keep quiet; we hoped you'd forgotten us
but, sadly, it seems that you've already spotted us;
hunted us down in your flash Mitsubishis,
fully convinced that you're saving our species.

I suppose our loud mating calls drew you tonight,
but you have to admit that it isn't polite
to shove cameras and microphones up our extremities
and label us 'pond-life' and other obscenities.

If you're planning to study our habits, you should
at the very least show some respect for our mud,
as you squelch and you splatter and slither around
in your wellies and moan. This is our stamping ground.

And it isn't just me; there are rather a lot of us
reckon it's getting a trifle monotonous
hearing you whinge and complain that it's soggy.
We like it: we chose it because it was boggy.

TROUT IN A TOP HAT
Susan Rogerson

Something most peculiar has happened here today,
The normal rules of nature have completely gone astray.
I saw an orange trout as I was walking into town,
He was wearing silk pyjamas and a purple dressing gown.
He smiled and doffed his hat to me, and said 'How do you do?
'I'm going to see an elephant who's caught the rabbit 'flu.'
He whistled as he strode away, and shouted out 'Good luck!'
As a badger on a skateboard started quacking like a duck.

I walked into the butcher's, where blue pigs were selling pies,
I asked them what was in them but they cried 'It's a surprise!'
So cautiously I took a bite, then spat it out again –
It was a brood of fluffy chicks, and irate mother hen.

continued ▶

POETRY FOR PERFORMANCE

◀ *TROUT IN A TOP HAT by Susan Rogerson*

She chased me down the street until I turned tomato red,
Then a bunch of pink bananas whacked me squarely round the head.

As I came to, a little dazed, and feeling rather sick,
I wondered – Was it in my mind? – Had I imagined it?
But then I looked above me, and could scarce believe my eyes –
A thousand pea-green kangaroos were dancing through the skies.
I struggled up and leant against a yellow-spotted tree,
Where a flock of angry penguins sat growling down at me.
I raced indoors, quite terrified; my heart all of a-flutter,
But waiting was a giant worm, who ate me for his supper.

SURFING SPIDER
Karen Pailing

I found you where the moon's soft light
lit up your web site late last night:
those silky threads your own home-spun
trapeze. I thought you might have run;
you froze, but still you made a stand,
inspecting every silver strand
for damage to the filigree
so carelessly disturbed by me.
You've claimed as yours the space between
the printer cable and the screen,
as though you plan to surf the net
you're guarding with your silhouette.

But, though you'll scuttle down below,
my spyware's onto you: I know
your browsing habits, and I'll bet
that, though we haven't caught you yet,
we will, when you're preoccupied
with menus, and you can't decide
between mosquitoes a) and b);
we'll take the opportunity

POETRY FOR PERFORMANCE

◀ *SURFING SPIDER by Karen Pailing*

to sweep away your home; no more
will windows, walls, the office door,
be shoulder-surfing-spider-patterned,
for soon you'll be debugged and flattened

LITTLE BROTHER
Ros Woolner

When we were seven, you were five
and liked to tag along.
We didn't want you trailing us,
but what we did was wrong.
The River Thames had burst its banks,
the field was now a lake
and we were wading further out –
towards our big mistake.
Our wellies were just tall enough
to keep the water out,
but your red boots were not as high:
'Please wait!' we heard you shout.
We stood you on a picnic bench,
an island high and dry,
then ran without a backward glance
and left you there to cry.
Back then, we thought it served you right –
your fault for being there.
Our lesson was: leave us alone;
you learned we did not care.
Though several years have passed since then

continued ▶

POETRY FOR PERFORMANCE

◀ *LITTLE BROTHER by Ros Woolner*

and things are not the same
(you know I care by now, I hope),
I still feel that old shame.
I left my brother, five years old,
abandoned in the flood,
showed not a drop of sympathy
for my own flesh and blood.
I'm sorry, wish I could rewind,
unthink, unsay, undo,
and offer you a piggy back –
take better care of you.

MERE WORDS
Kelly Davis

Half-remembered words of songs,
Words of love, words of hate.
Whispered words of hope – and fear.
Words that fall upon deaf ears.

Words as weapons,
Words on banners:
'Not right! Not fair!'
Words that hang in the air.

Sugared words of romance.
Words that sully innocence.
Words that touch the heart
Words that tear you apart.

Wily, weasel words.
Hollow words that miss their mark.
Too many words – and too few actions,
Glib words and kneejerk reactions.

POETRY FOR PERFORMANCE

◀ *MERE WORDS by Kelly Davis*

Sometimes words pile up,
And choke us with their papery wings.
Fine words from forked tongues
Cloud our minds, clog our lungs.

Yet – finding the right words,
To say what we mean,
Could still change everything…

BEACHCOMBING
Alison Chisholm

Have you seen them there at the tideline?
Each swell of water drops
a row of random treasures at your feet,
coke cans glistening in the sun,
a baby's dummy
with sparkling crust of salt.

Single sandals suggest someone had to hop,
abandoned T shirts that they went
bare-chested. Plastic spades and buckets
might have been discarded
when a sandcastle was patted into shape,
while orange peel and tinfoil salute
the messiness of picnickers.

Have you seen, too, sea's detritus?
Abandoned homes of shells,
cameo pink, bleached white, and indigo,
stud the rocks. Here a shark's tooth
has lost its power to terrify; there
a dead crab brittles in the heat.

continued ▶

POETRY FOR PERFORMANCE

◀ *BEACHCOMBING by Alison Chisholm*

Seaweed strands
still have their oily tang,
and sloughed-off mermaids' purses cluster.

All this makes you a witness
to the ocean's parallel world;
for everything you see
has its story, its history, its legend.
These things, their tales, are yours for the taking,
gifts offered and replenished with every tide,
water's presents to the land. Enjoy.

14 YEARS AND ABOVE

THE SHORT VIEW
Ali Pickford

If I were going to die next week
I'd thank my mum and dad
For all the hot dinners
And good times that we've had

If I were going to die next week
I'd put my house in order
Clear up all my books and junk
I'd stop being such a hoarder

I'd read the letters that I've kept
Then shut them up and box them tight
Not wasting one more moment
Holding things now out of sight

I'd be kinder with other people's hearts
Guard them with crystal care
I'd hope they'd do the same to me
If I lay my soul bare

continued ▶

POETRY FOR PERFORMANCE

◀ *THE SHORT VIEW by Ali Pickford*

I might worry less
And live more
Take less
I'd give more

I might wish less
And pray more
Regret less
Forgive more

I'd kiss the boy
I'd book the trips
Enjoy the fact
I've curvy hips…

I'd let go of the past
Be free at last
Forgive quicker
Forget fast.

14 YEARS AND ABOVE

I hope I'm not going to die next week
Or tomorrow, or today
But come to think of it…
I might start doing all that anyway

Because if I were going to die tomorrow
I might start living today.

GOOSEBERRIES
Lynne Sutton

The pedals spin wildly,
clattering
and whirring
as I throw down my bike
on a burgeoning verge
of the country lane.

Toes in scuffed sandals
scrabble for a hold
until I am braced by scraped knees
and balanced on tree-stained
T-shirt belly across our neighbour's
garden wall.

Reaching for the arching branches
of spread, green leaves, my grubby fingers
hunt the dark spaces beneath them,
ignoring the thorns
that catch at my bare arms
leaving dot-and-dash snags.

14 YEARS AND ABOVE

The heavy jewels of berries
cluster in striped and hairy
white-green weight
and I pull them off one by one
to cram them
into my grimacing mouth.

Sourness shrivels my tongue
as teeth split the tough resistance
of each thick-bristled skin.
The sweetness of seeds is swallowed quickly -
what I want is the eye-watering
acidity of the slow-chewed rind.

An angry shout and cracking of walking-stick
tip on the garden-path bricks
reaches my straining ears
and I snatch one last glorious,
gleefully illicit goosegog
before I can be caught,

then hoik up my bike
through a tug of stinging
nettles and pedal away

continued ▶

◀ *GOOSEBERRIES by Lynne Sutton*

as fast and free as the wind
but with the beginnings
of belly-ache.

ONE DAY
Emma-Louise Tinniswood

One day I'll remember
When this war has waged her last,
And winds have blown away the sounds
When they echo in the past.
One day I'll remember, how it felt
To sit with you and stare,
And breathe the summer scents without
The fear of death that's there.

One day I'll remember
Without the tears that cloud my eyes,
How it felt to hold your hand and look
Up at bright blue skies.
How it felt to laugh and smile
In carefree happy ways,
Without the sounds that pierce my ears
That took my love away.

Perhaps in many years to come,
My powerless heart will cease
To fill my ears with a heavy beat

continued ▶

POETRY FOR PERFORMANCE

◀ *ONE DAY by Emma-Louise Tinniswood*

And find some small release
From all the dreams and imaginings,
Of what my mind has seen.
Perhaps one day I'll find I wake
And realise that isn't a dream.

Perhaps one day I'll touch the sand
Without you standing there.
Or paddle my feet by the bridge we loved
Without your fingers in my hair;
And maybe one day when we all can breathe
And feel the silence again,
I'll sit by the window at the desk you gave
And take up paper and pen.

One day in the summer perhaps we'll meet once more,
And as I hold your picture close
I try to imagine what you saw.
I try to feel how you must have felt,
What this war put you through.
One day in the winter,
Perhaps I'll come to you.

14 YEARS AND ABOVE

A HURRIED CONFESSION
Freya Carroll

I've got to make this quick
because
There's not much time left
because
You're leaving in an hour
because
Your stupid mother wants to live abroad
which
Is really thick when you think about it
I mean
Why live abroad when you could live here
I mean
People speak English here
And
They don't abroad
but
I'm sorry
Don't go
I'll spit it out

continued ▶

◀ *A HURRIED CONFESSION by Freya Carroll*

So
I just wanted to say
that
There's something about you
that
Only you seem to have
I mean
I've looked for it in other people
But
No one seems to have that kind of spark you do
Yes
I know it's confusing
And
I don't really get it myself
And
It's kind of your fault
I mean
You don't have to be like this
And –
I'm sorry
I'll get on with it

14 YEARS AND ABOVE

Sorry

I think it's your eyes
Not
The size
Because
They're really large
(Do you know that? I mean, they're like a puppy's eyes, except you're a human, and a puppy's a puppy but either way it's kind of cute)
It's not the colour
Because
They're just blue
(And really, really blue, do you wear contacts or something because they are just far too blue to exist I mean wow)
It's this kind of shine
And
That's really cheesy
But
It's kind of beautiful

I know you don't ever look at me
Although

continued ▶

POETRY FOR PERFORMANCE

◀ *A HURRIED CONFESSION by Freya Carroll*

I sit next to you in Physics

And

I steal your pencils

(The brown one's the colour of your hair)

You don't look at me

And

That's fine

I know you have to go

Like

Right now

Like

You should have left five minutes ago

And

Your mum's getting stressy

But

I just wanted to say

That

I love you.

That's all.

PRICELESS
Freya Carroll

My name is Amy, and I am worth £507.56

Which is not as much as Peter Nathan, who is worth £990

(He's the mayor's son)

But it's a nice number to be worth

And so I like it.

I go to school.

In history they teach us about the Olden Days

When their Olden Days was our Ancient Days

(Which is so long ago)

And when they sent people to jail

And everything was confusing.

In Free they teach us things to make us worth more

Like cooking and cleaning

Even though Free technically means 'free learning'

And cooking and cleaning don't help at all

(Even if Josephine says she was worth a whole six pence more after she learnt to cook crème brulee)

In Art

(That's where I met you, remember?)

They don't teach us at all,

And we can relax.

continued ▶

POETRY FOR PERFORMANCE

◀ *A HURRIED CONFESSION by Freya Carroll*

I like relaxing.
And in Assembly we look at pictures of people who are worth thousands.
I am not worth thousands.
I am worth £507.56,
Which is a nice number to be worth,
And I like it.
Sometimes, I don't like it,
And I cry at night while the tramps (who are worth only 50p) and the alley cats (tabbies £8.30 other breeds £5) wail outside.
Sometimes, I don't like it,
And I don't pay attention in history and free and assembly, not even in Art,
I just stare at the expensive ones and learn to hate instead.
But.
You are worth £492.44
And together we make one thousand
(More than Peter Nathan)
And that is good enough for me.

14 YEARS AND ABOVE

HEARING THE ECHOES
Kelly Davis

In the museum, we each choose an object.
I select a small piece of ancient cement,
greyish-brown and gritty on one side,
smooth and painted on the other.

I close my eyes and warm it in my hand:
skin to stone, present to past.
I listen, and the lifeless lump
clears its dusty throat:

'I slept while the river washed me –
gently when it trickled in the spring,
violently in its winter spate –
until a Roman mason scooped me up.

He mixed me with sand, ash and gravel,
studded me with chips of black and brown,
and spread me on a villa wall,
leaving me to dry and harden.

continued ▶

POETRY FOR PERFORMANCE

◀ *HEARING THE ECHOES by Kelly Davis*

Soon a painter came,
sucked his teeth and dipped his brush
in cream and terracotta,
painted me in careful bands of colour.

A young Roman officer set up home
with his dark-haired, pregnant wife.
Children were born and grew.
The officer's face grew lined.

Years passed, the people vanished.
The roof fell in, the rain washed me.
I watched a family of fox cubs play,
and felt the pull of the soil.

Centuries piled up, one after another.
I slept beneath my brown blankets,
dreaming of water, fire, men and women.
Then something shifted, and I woke.

14 YEARS AND ABOVE

A trowel loosened the earth above me,
a brush dusted the crumbs away.
I was lifted into the blinding light:
a painful, joyous rebirth.

Just now, your hand hovered,
reached down and chose me.
You listened,
and I could speak.'

SEAGULL'S 'SWOOPING ATTACK' IN MARYPORT DELAYS MAIL DELIVERY
Kelly Davis

Every day you patrolled our street,
        defending your adolescent chicks,
who squatted, plump, on two parked cars,
        awaiting their next food parcel.

Children, adults, people bringing letters,
        You terrorised us all.
You were even 'mentioned in dispatches'.

One day I forgot your presence
        and foolishly strolled past your chimney roost.
Your face a furious paper cutout,
        you plummeted earthwards.

I swore and flinched
        as your armoured claws skimmed my scalp,
your wingfeather quills speared the air.

14 YEARS AND ABOVE

I heard your harpy shriek,
        sensed your yellow eye lasering my skull,
felt a membrane tear
        between my world and yours.

A millisecond before skull contact,
        you fired a Jackson Pollock splat right down
          my back –
a gooey archipelago of khaki, brown and white.

Weeks passed. One chick died, the other grew,
and finally you left for somewhere new.
Your lofty fortress stands empty.
The battle has ended –
for now.

TRIBAL VOICES
Kelly Davis

The TV journalist talks
above the many tongues,
guttural, choking, sibilant, stuttering,
then singles out the one who speaks good English.
Some of the women wear headscarves.
The men have baseball caps, jeans and mobile phones.
They look like us but sound so different.

Meanwhile, Facebook babbles its binary language:
extremist outbursts,
emojis and emoticons,
the Me, Me, Me,
the Them and Us,
the pus
that oozes just beneath our European skin.

We whisper to each other,
feed our fears, cover our ears,
hug ourselves a little tighter,
watch them on our screens,
sinking in their dinghies,

14 YEARS AND ABOVE

screaming, weeping,
shoving babies through train windows.

After months of media reports
their collective grief becomes white noise,
until a single picture
scissors through
the blanket coverage.
A Turkish policeman carries a child's limp body,
the tiny shoes pointing down.

MR FALSTAFF
David Madison

'Mr Falstaff,' scoffed the squirrel, 'Tell me why you sleep all day?'
But Falstaff merely doffed his cap, continued on his way.
'Oh Falstaff, you're a lazy boy!' squealed Marjorie the Trout.
But Falstaff out of courtesy refrained from speaking out.
They accuse, who have no shoes,
He mused mysteriously;
With head held high, I'll walk on by,
And they can sigh and wonder why;
But shoeless I'll not be.

'Poor Falstaff, such a wasted life!' jeered Polly Parakeet.
But Falstaff gave a little bow and turned the other cheek.
'Get up!' implored the buffalo, 'Get up for all our sakes!'
But Falstaff smiled and persevered in purchasing cream cakes.
They mock, they mock, they have no socks,

He said sagaciously;
I'm damp of nose, with eighteen toes,
Let them suppose I doze and doze –
This life of idleness I chose;
But sockless I'll not be.

'Mr Falstaff,' moaned the monkey, 'Show a little bit of
 care!'
But Falstaff simply carried on attending to his hair.
'Think you' declared the weasel 'that the world round
 you revolves?'
But Falstaff coughed politely and refused to get
 involved.
They chastise, who don't wear ties,
Was his philosophy.
My life is mine, I find it fine –
I like to dine on cheese and wine;
So let them whine that it's a crime,
I'll stay in line and bide my time;
But tieless I'll not be!

FLOATING
Susan Rogerson

Five hundred pink balloons rise above the city smoke,
Five hundred nylon strings attaching messages of hope.
The people are uplifted as they watch them float away,
They point and laugh, then turn their backs, and get on with their day.
And far removed in time and space, balloons begin to burst,
And all the people's hopes and dreams plummet back to earth.

They scatter over hills and fields like alien confetti,
Their strings a knot of tangled snakes to capture the unwary.
They snag among the treetops, in permanent suspension,
Grotesque, deformed baubles from some gothic high convention.
And some of them are floating still, but now float on the seas,
Buoys to mark the tragedy unfolding deep beneath.

A stately old leviathan, browsing for his supper,
Sees a bright pink jellyfish, just like any other.
His shell cannot protect him from the twisting pain inside,
Listless, swimming aimlessly, confusion in his eyes.
He cannot eat, his body weak, he struggles hard for breath,
His world is out of focus, all he longs for now is rest.

Carried by the currents, his mind begins to drift,
Floating, floating, on and on, through seas of jellyfish.
And soon this noble giant, of one hundred years or more,
Is just another body, washed up on the shore.

OUT, DAMNED SPOT
Susan Rogerson

'What,
'will these hands ne'er be clean?'
Lady MacBeth's words
ring in her ears
as she scrubs; scrubs,
each finger in turn,
under every nail –
mustn't miss a speck
or she'll have to start again.

Sunlight floods her stage,
birds sing their chorus
as she plunges her miserable demons
into the soapy, scalding abyss –
waves of lathered heat
sucking her breath;
face pricked with sweat –
hands seared, blood-red.

Sounds of summer drift
through the open window:

14 YEARS AND ABOVE

a mower thrumming;
children laughing;
the drone of a light plane –
Is she going insane?

Hands; wrists; arms;
knuckles; palms;
a spiralling wall of thoughts
encases her brain –
circling her skull
like the tower of Dunsinane.

Daggers' twist
through the whispering dark.
Ravens caw her name.
Her soul screams.

She claws at iron
till her mind bleeds.

How she longs
to smash these shackles;
run from her dank dungeon
into sweet, clean air;

continued ▶

POETRY FOR PERFORMANCE

◀ *OUT, DAMNED SPOT by Susan Rogerson*

feel the sun's warmth on her face.

But Fear and Doubt – her jailors,
keep her chained –
washing away imaginary sins;
tortured by thoughts of what might have been –
Lady MacBeth's words
forever ringing in her ears…

14 YEARS AND ABOVE

PLEASE WILL SOMEONE FEED THE CAT?

Susan Rogerson

She stares at the old woman in the chair,
head lolled in sleep; hollow-cheeked;
the cat miaowing round her legs,
desperate to be fed.
His plaintive cries make her want to weep,
but no tears will ever fall again.

Tattered curtains bar the day,
sunlight fails to penetrate the grime.
The television prattles to itself,
the light bulb flickering in time.
And the cat miaows; his green eyes plead,
she struggles with the cupboard door in vain –
the tins remain locked inside.
Why doesn't anyone come by?

His water bowl is dry.
He licks the dripping tap, tries to catch a fly
bashing against the window pane –
but it slips out of reach, crawls through a hole

continued ▶

POETRY FOR PERFORMANCE

◀ *PLEASE WILL SOMEONE FEED THE CAT by Susan Rogerson*

in the rotting frame.
She grapples with the latch, but it's stuck tight,
the light bulb rings, tings, blinks out.

The cat miaows through the dark
and her heart breaks –
Can't anyone hear his cries?

Blue light dances on the old woman's face,
shifting shadows in the gloom,
as the television prattles to itself.
The cat is thin and weak –
he can't jump up to the kitchen sink
so he lies down at the old woman's feet
and closes his eyes.

Her anguished cries make no sound,
Why hasn't anyone come by?

A knock; a ring; a shout; an almighty crash –
two hard circles of light pierce the black.

14 YEARS AND ABOVE

Strangers in her home
pull collars over nose and mouth –
curtains are peeled back and light floods in.

They stare at the old woman in the chair,
and the cat, asleep at her feet,
and shake their heads and sigh,
then flick the television switch.

And the old woman calls to her cat,
and they leave, side by side.

RECAPTURING THE MAGIC
Susan Rogerson

Oberon, you bog-brained fool! You rotting peach!
Will you sit upon that spotted stool all day –
slug-slime-glued? I've leaves to hoover up!
Rancid butter-blob – shift your fungus-feet!

Cease, withered croak-frog! Can't a man have peace
to read the Faery Star in his own home,
without your vixen's bleats; your she-owl screech?
Away you scratch-cat – leave your king alone!

Away to where, my Lord? The woods are scarce
and we are forced by shameful circumstance
to live as paupers on this roundabout –
our Trains all gone, except for loyal Pease.

Have I not kept you safe from ash disease,
so fatal to a faery's tiny lungs;
these trees protected by our tarmac moat?
No humans here disturb our spritely dreams.

Feckless toad! We're here because you sank
our faery dust in tree-funds – now collapsed.
And don't these traffic fumes burn just as strong,
and tar my dainty tubes and cause this cough?

It's not my fault the record mast crashed markets,
and acorns hit rock-bottom – do not chide!
Besides, what's wrong with living quietly now?
We're far too old to gallivant! Tee… you listening?

Bottom… Now there was an ass: loyal and true –
Remember that enchanted night, so long ago,
of merry mischief; muddled love; much ado?
Oh, Obe, let's fly tonight – relive our sweet youth!

Daft rere-mouse – have you beetle eggs for brains?
You know my wings are wormy as the grave!
Though I confess Dear, I've fond memories
of such sweet-scented Love-in-idleness.

Then ring the bluebell for Pease – bid him fetch
a skein of silver thread from spider's web,
and finest needle of pine. I'll mend your wings
my Love – and I've scrimped a little faery dust –

continued ▶

POETRY FOR PERFORMANCE

◀ *RECAPTURING THE MAGIC by Susan Rogerson*

My precious Love! Fox-wise, yet sweet as musk-rose!
I'll check out Elfbook, see what's trending now.
We'll cast our spell on unsuspecting humans –
Tonight, my Faery Queen, we'll reign once more!

SUFFOCATION
Susan Rogerson

Once I lived in the wild place,
under a warm sun,
free to run, and laugh, and sing.

Then I was locked in a cage,
where strangers masquerading as friends
told me I couldn't sing,
laughed at my laugh.
So I lost my voice.

I was mauled,
till I curled up in a tight little ball
and hid my face –
longing for the wild place.

Then one day I escaped.
I ran and ran
but there were chains around my legs.
The further I ran, the more they weighed me down,
till I could only crawl
back to the wild place.

continued ▶

◀ *SUFFOCATION by Susan Rogerson*

But it had changed.
There was no sun –
only wind and rain and cold.
I shivered
and the chains cut into my legs
till the blood ran.

So cold.
I found a place to hide –
warm and dry –
where I could watch the wild place.

But my hide was just another cage,
and though the door was open wide
I remained trapped inside.

And the walls squeezed in
till I couldn't see the wild place,
except in my dreams.

They squeezed

until there was no room for dreams.

Squeezed
until I couldn't move –

couldn't breathe.

THE LOLLIPOP TREE
Susan Rogerson

In a faraway land, the lollipop tree
stands all alone on a wide grassy bank.
Its hard, shiny fruits sparkle and dance,
and clink in the breeze, which wafts the sweet scent,
to tease and to tempt, until everyone wants
a lollipop from the lollipop tree.

But before it lies a vast, black swamp,
circled with reeds, all slimy and rank;
shrouded with clouds of sulphurous steam,
blupping with bubbles, bright yellow and green.
But the people plunge in, for all they can see
is the jingling-jangling lollipop tree.

They splash through the soup like a wildebeest herd,
pushing and shoving – all fight to be first.
But midges swarm round and bite at their backs,
while under the surface weeds are amassed –
green-fronded serpents that coil tightly round
susceptible legs, till some flounder and drown –
but the herd surges on without looking around.

14 YEARS AND ABOVE

And right in the middle the water is deep,
and crocodiles lurk for the sick and the weak.
Jaws clamp around necks in a final death-roll,
but the herd stumbles onwards, all eyes on their goal.
They scramble the bank and start laughing with glee
at the spingling-spangling lollipop tree.

They race for the lollies; grab fistfuls of fruit –
stuff faces; stuff pockets; stuff suitcases, boots.
They clamber on branches and beat them with sticks,
till the ground around's littered with leaves and
  snapped twigs.
And when it's stripped bare they cart off their prize,
and the lollipop tree slowly withers and dies.

They pile all their loot onto small wooden boats,
and set sail for home – too heavy to float.
And swamp-men appear from out of the depths
with cold, clammy hands and hot, foetid breath.
They tip the boats up till the lollipops fall
into the mire - to a great caterwaul.

continued ▶

POETRY FOR PERFORMANCE

◀ *THE LOLLIPOP TREE by Susan Rogerson*

Hands scrabble in vain as lollipops bob
out of their reach and sink into the mud.
And some are so frantic to regain their haul,
they leap from the boats - and don't surface at all.
While battered survivors stagger to land,
broken and bruised, to collapse on the ground.

They survey the carnage strewn in the bog,
water-blown corpses, drifting through fog;
bumping the debris caught in the reeds;
blupping with gases; slimy and green.
And the blingling-blangling lollipop tree
is now just a sticky-sweet memory.

But from somewhere over the vast, black swamp,
in a faraway land, on a wide, grassy bank,
there drifts the faint sound of a tinkling tree,
with sweet-scented fruits that waft in the breeze,
disguising the vapours that rise through the reeds;
fragrancing nostrils, they tempt and they tease,
till the pong is forgotten and everyone needs
a lollipop from the lollipop tree.

CRASH
Amy Shearer

This morning I rode the bus to work
Trailed my eyes out of the window and thought about
   the usual
Until the High Road
Where the traffic turned strange
Vacated lanes
And rush-hour people standing still
Staring at something

The bus driver slowed to a crawl
And then started talking
Oh god a crash
Oh god
A crash
And there's the car
It's upside down my god
And the driver
The driver is still inside
She's stuck
And there's blood on the windscreen, oh my god

◀ *CRASH by Amy Shearer*

And the passengers stood up to see
Went to the crash side of the bus and craned their necks
And the driver slowed even more to get a good look at the broken girl
His voice talking faster and louder about the metal trapping her and the sharded glass all over her and her blood coming out of her

I wanted him to SHUT HIS MOUTH and take us away
This bus full of poking eyes
Don't look at her like that
Don't look
Don't look unless you can save her

14 YEARS AND ABOVE

PINK EYE/STINK EYE IN SAN FRANCISCO
Amy Shearer

(Note: In American English, 'pink eye' refers to conjunctivitis; 'stink eye' means 'dirty look'.)

Strange sleep came out of my left eye this morning
So I went to the doctor
Here's some medication
She said
You have pink eye
Very contagious

Pink eye
I thought
Reminds me of little piglets

I got on the bus to go home
Sat down, before I realized it, next to a very stroppy
   woman complaining to herself
But out loud
Because she wanted us to hear
Because she wanted it to be our fault

continued ▶

◀ *PINK EYE/STINK EYE IN SAN FRANCISCO by Amy Shearer*

Yer ciddy is garbage

She said

Yer transit system is garbage

She said

It's impaaaahssible to get anywhere

Impaaahssible

Pause

Eye rolls

White eye

I looked down at my book

Best not make eye-contact with the talkers

And I wasn't in the mood, what with the pink eye and all

Yes yer ciddy is garrbage garrbage

Do you hear me?

I looked up again

As she seemed to be addressing me

The nearest on hand

14 YEARS AND ABOVE

And by the time this bus finally gets there?
She said
The whole place will be full of immigrants who can't even speak English!
I can't take it
More eye rolls

Are you talking to me?
I asked
Because I don't want you to

She gave me the stink eye
On the East Coast we have subways
She said

We have a subway
I said

You do naaaht have a subway
She said
The EAST COAST has subways
(As if this meant there weren't any left for us)

continued ▶

POETRY FOR PERFORMANCE

◀ *PINK EYE/STINK EYE IN SAN FRANCISCO by Amy Shearer*

Feel free to return to the East Coast
I said
As soon as you like

She didn't answer
Looked purposefully weary and off-stage left

I rubbed my pink eye in her direction, hoping to
 contage her

At Market and Church she got up to get off
Tried again to make it all our fault, our city, our transit,
 our garbage, our immigrants
While on the East Coast they have subways!

We drove away from her

That's why we have an East Coast and West Coast
Said a man on the bus
So that we can all be happy

14 YEARS AND ABOVE

The bus laughed, relieved

He was quite a nice-looking man actually
I smiled and closed my pink eye away from him, so as
  not to contage
He winked at me
Brown eye

MAUREEN, IN HER CHAIR
Kelly Davis

'Yes', 'No', 'Hello', 'I think so'.
These are her only words.
Unimaginable – but so it is.
One side of her body paralysed;
her world shrunk to a window;
a woman who used to ponder consciousness
is discussed by others:
How does she feel? How can we know?
Inside her brain, neurons take aim, tremble –
and miss their targets.
Words ricochet
and shatter into stuttered syllables.

The first night of the holiday in Scotland:
one moment standing by the sink,
the next horizontal.
Normal life slipping
into something so unutterably different.
'It would have killed most people,' the doctors said.
But exercise and healthy eating had buttressed her
 heart,

and weeks of hospital treatment finally delivered her
to the care of a devoted daughter;
back to her home,
where everything – and nothing –
was the same.

Once she strode the fells.
Now, crossing the room
requires tight-lipped effort.
From her chair, she watches the starlings.
They squawk and shriek
in their busy battles.
Tired now, she dozes,
watches daytime TV,
wishes she could read a book,
string a sentence,
bridge the chasm,
from mind to mouth.

There are irritations:
the magazine splayed on the coffee table,
the breadcrumbs freckling the kitchen counter.
She was always tidy.
Now she must sit back;

continued ▶

POETRY FOR PERFORMANCE

◀ *MAUREEN, IN HER CHAIR by Kelly Davis*

no longer acting
but acted upon.
It's not all gloom.
The house is warm.
We drift and gather, talk and laugh.
She smiles and nods,
Still the loving mother and grandmother.

The carers come at their appointed hours.
But every visit ends.
The silence turns into a tinnitus scream.
Friends, children, grandchildren
leave to pursue their lives,
out in the frenetic world,
while Maureen stays in her chair,
wrapped in her shawl of memories.
There she waits
for the minutes, hours, days, to pass.
Accepting what is
and whatever comes next —

14 YEARS AND ABOVE

LIFE IN THE OLD DOG
Kelly Davis

All week you have laboured,
Occasionally winching yourself
Up to a standing position
To drink or pee.

Eating is a burden.
Mostly you turn away.
But we coax you to eat a mouthful
Now and then.

Reduced to a bag of fur,
Sometimes barely breathing,
You seem to melt
Into the floor.

With sunken flank and cloudy eye,
You are now mere essence of dog,
But still twitch
When we stroke you.

POETRY FOR PERFORMANCE

◀ *LIFE IN THE OLD DOG by Kelly Davis*

Poor old soldier, each day we wake,
Half-expecting to find your corpse.
But the little flag keeps fluttering,
Not yet ready to surrender.

The sun warmed you yesterday
While you lay on the grass.
The wind combed your fur
And sang you to sleep.

Stretched on the carpet now,
Your front paws are still bent,
As if running
Through a dreamscape.

MERMAID
Susan Rogerson

Perched on her rock, she combs her sticky hair;
dark droplets form an oil slick down her back.
Where once the dolphins tumbled, now she stares
at bloodless ocean, dressed in mourning black –
carrier bags lit up in stark relief
by U.V. rays that blot her marbled flesh.
She longs to smell the seagrass round the reef;
race marlin through the storm waves, melt-ice fresh.
She tugs a wrack of plastic from her tail,
wincing as she feels the angler's barb
embedded deep beneath her scabby scales –
she squeezes yellow pus from weeping scars.

An engine throbs; she slips back into scum,
then holds her breath and dives beyond the sun.

WHEN FORTY YEARS HAVE PASSED
Kelly Davis

When forty years have passed and done their worst,
And lines appear upon your forehead fair,
Your peachy skin that now looks fit to burst,
Will bunch and sag like clothes too big to wear.
That faddy diet will leave you skin and bone,
Your blood will slow and gradually grow cold.
You may then ask where all your beauty's flown.
What happened to the pin-up looks of old?
A pile of selfies may be all that's left;
Not much, it seems, for all there is to show
Of life – with all its twists, its warp and weft.
Nothing is reaped by those who never sow.
  To bear a child might well have kept you young,
  A ball of life towards the future flung.

THE SPIDER AND THE FLY
Susan Rogerson

I am the careless fly that stumbled blindly,
straight into your web of silken thread.
You tied your sticky noose around me finely,
I did not feel your poison in my head.
Your velvet venom coursed through every vein,
curdled my sweet blood and turned it blue.
My life-force, once so strong, began to drain,
my body and my soul sucked out by you.
Powerless against your toxic potion,
I did not try to struggle, but remained
lying helpless, dying in slow motion,
accepting that my fate was pre-ordained.
Till dried up; desiccated; mummified,
you plucked me from your web; tossed me aside.

EMBERS

Kelly Davis

The burning embers lying in a fire
Must all transmute to ash to feed the flame.
So humble bricks pile up to build a spire.
If no one loses, no one wins the game.
In life is death, the ghost within the child.
The mirror does not lie; the years will pass,
Through summers warm, and winters chill and wild,
Till all that is becomes no more than grass.
You may believe you are a special case,
The rules of time do not apply to you.
That might seem true when youth glows in your face
But later on you'll find you're in a queue.
For what, you ask? One hopes, a peaceful death,
And – say it soft – an easy final breath.

JESSICA

Kelly Davis

The water laps against the stone below,
The city rings with sounds of drum and fife.
What lies ahead? I fear I do not know.
Is it a sin to crave another life?
My father vows to keep me locked in tight,
I yearn to leave this dark and airless place.
I am resolved; tonight I will take flight
And leave behind my creed, my faith, my race.
The box of ducats heavy in my hand,
My heart almost as heavy in my chest.
Against all sense, the flame of love is fanned,
But will my lover pass or fail the test?
After this night, nothing will be the same.
Too late for doubts, I hear him call my name.

SERPENT'S TONGUE: A RESPONSE TO SHAKESPEARE'S SONNET 147

Susan Rogerson

If I am dark as night, you made me so,
as sure as snake that mesmerizes shrew;
you rooted me to earth, then struck your blow:
forked promises of love, forever true.
As burning venom paralysed my heart,
your velvet coils enveloped my soft skin;
my sweet blood crushed till vessels burst apart,
and flung my artless mind in deathly spin.
My rosy cheeks blanched white – all goodness drained,
bright flame consumed, my body warped with cold;
black, shrivelled soul: Hell's ash – while all you gained
was marble sculpture, carved in your foul mould.
Your serpent's love turned mine to polished hate –
now poison's fire bites inward – seals your fate.

WHO CAN KNOW?
Susan Cartwright-Smith

Who can know what will bewitch and charm,
What curl of lip, what curl of hair, what face
Will make one person fall, another chase
A different soul? What makes one person calm
Another may not to that visage warm.
If this is it, we are alone in space
And godless rocks do drift and soar and race,
The choices here on earth should not alarm –
Our life is fleeting. Happiness is all.
To find a kindred spirit once or twice
In life, you see, can only add some spice
To dishes dull. Our minds reach out and call
Beyond our loins' brisk tossing of the dice.
Connection, Love – can break down any walls.

THE BOTTOM OF THE JAR
Susan Cartwright-Smith

I tried to reach the bottom of the jar
Without touching the stickiness of the rim.
The long spoon, devil-supper, sticky as tar
From old treacle crusted, greasy, black and grim.
I'm loathe to admit defeat, be bested,
But to open a fresh new jar appeals.
Shall I persevere? Be sorely tested,
By the disgust and the distaste of how it feels.
So it is when I see you beside me,
The conflict of the new becoming old.
To touch you feels familiar, should excite me
But my fingers and my heart are growing cold.
To struggle with the old despite distaste
When it would be so easy to replace.

ACKNOWLEDGEMENTS

For permission to print the copyright material in this anthology, we make grateful acknowledgement to the following authors:

Buxton, Amy *Louisa And The Field Mouse* Used by permission of Amy Buxton • **Carroll, Freya** *A Hurried Confession; Priceless* Used by permission of Freya Carroll • **Cartwright-Smith, Susan** *Who Can Know?; The Bottom Of The Jar* Used by permission of Susan Cartwright-Smith • **Chisholm, Alison** *In The Rain; Byron Tries To Knit; Beachcombing* Used by permission of Alison Chisholm • **Davis, Kelly** *Mere Words; Hearing The Echoes; Seagull's Swooping Attack; Tribal Voices; Maureen, In Her Chair; Life In The Old Dog; When Forty Years Have Passed; Embers; Jessica* Used by permission of Kelly Davis • **Dean, Peter** *Natural Autumn* Used by permission of Peter Dean • **Goldberg, Harris** *Crabs* Used by permission of Harris Goldberg • **Harding, Anne** *Dead Bird Talking* Used by permission of Anne Harding • **Lees, Sylvia** *Barnabas And Me; Odd Footprints On An Empty Beach* Used by permission of Sylvia Lees • **Loughrey, Anita** *The Fairground; Spider In The Classroom* Used by permission of Anita Loughrey • **Maddison, David** *Mr Falstaff* © The Playing Space • **Maddocks, Gabi** *My Favourite Colour; Tangled Laces; Maybe One Day; Late; What Lies Beyond* © The Playing Space • **Pailing, Karen** *Uncle Bernie's Beard; Looking Out; Natterjack; Surfing Spider* Used by

ACKNOWLEDGEMENTS

permission of Karen Pailing • **Pickford, Ali** *The Short View* Used by permission of Ali Pickford • **Rogerson, Susan** *Harvest Supper; Dear Father Christmas; The Country Squire; Trout In A Top Hat; Floating; Out, Damned Spot; Please Will Someone Feed The Cat?; Recapturing The Magic; Suffocation; The Lollipop Tree; Mermaid; The Spider And The Fly; Serpent's Tongue* Used by permission of Susan Rogerson • **Shearer, Amy** *Crash; Pink Eye/Stink Eye In San Francisco* Used by permission of Amy Shearer • **Stevens, Sheila** *Zebra; Maximilian's Whale* Used by permission of Sheila Stevens • **Street, Zöe** *Cats* Used by permission of Zöe Street • **Sutton, Lynne** *Gooseberries* Used by permission of Lynne Sutton • **Tinniswood, Emma-Louise** *One Day* Used by permission of Emma-Louise Tinniswood • **Tomlinson, Shirley** *Aliens Under The Bed; A Very Scary Teacher* Used by permission of Shirley Tomlinson • **Whyte, Margaret** *On The Bridge* Used by permission of Margaret Whyte • **Wolfe, Emma** *The Giant; Witches; How To Terrify A Mole; Snake Meets Man* © The Playing Space • **Woolf, Alex** *There's Nothing Under The Bed* Used by permission of Alex Woolf • **Woolner, Ros** *Twirling, FIFA 17, Little Brother* Used by permission of Ros Woolner.

INDEX OF POETS

Buxton, Amy 17

Carroll, Freya 77, 81

Cartwright-Smith, Susan 127, 128

Chisholm, Alison 9, 24, 67

Davis, Kelly 65, 83, 86, 88, 116, 119, 122, 124, 125

Dean, Peter 38

Goldberg, Harris 6

Harding, Anne 52

Lees, Sylvia 19, 44

Loughrey, Anita 26, 54

Maddison, David 90

Maddocks, Gabi 15, 21, 28, 45, 49

Pailing, Karen 36, 42, 58, 61

Pickford, Ali 69

Rogerson, Susan 29, 47, 56, 59, 92, 94, 97, 100, 103, 106, 121, 123, 126

Shearer, Amy 109, 111

Stevens, Sheila 10, 34

Street, Zöe 7

Sutton, Lynne 72

Tinniswood, Emma-Louise 75

Tomlinson, Shirley 30, 32

◀ INDEX OF POETS

Whyte, Margaret 13

Wolfe, Emma 11, 12, 23, 51

Woolf, Alex 40

Woolner, Ros 14, 16, 63

INDEX OF TITLES

A Hurried Confession 77

A Very Scary Teacher 32

Aliens Under The Bed 30

Barnabas And Me 19

Beachcombing 67

Byron Tries To Knit 24

Cats 7

Crabs 6

Crash 109

Dead Bird Talking 52

Dear Father Christmas 47

Embers 124

FIFA 17 16

Floating 92

INDEX OF TITLES

Gooseberries 72

Harvest Supper 29

Hearing The Echoes 83

How To Terrify A Mole 23

In The Rain 9

Jessica 125

Late 45

Life In The Old Dog 119

Little Brother 63

Looking Out 42

Louisa And The Field Mouse 17

Maureen, In Her Chair 116

Maximilian's Whale 34

Maybe One Day 28

Mere Words 65

Mermaid 121

Mr Falstaff 90

My Favourite Colour 15

Natterjack 58

Natural Autumn 38

Odd Footprints On An Empty Beach 44

On The Bridge 13

One Day 75

Out, Damned Spot 94

POETRY FOR PERFORMANCE

◀ INDEX OF TITLES

Pink Eye/Stink Eye In San Francisco 111

Please Will Someone Feed The Cat? 97

Priceless 81

Recapturing The Magic 100

Seagull's Swooping Attack 86

Serpent's Tongue 126

Snake Meets Man 51

Spider In The Classroom 26

Suffocation 103

Surfing Spider 61

Tangled Laces 21

The Bottom Of The Jar 128

The Country Squire 56

The Fairground 54

The Giant 11

The Lollipop Tree 106

The Short View 69

The Spider And The Fly 123

There's Nothing Under The Bed 40

Tribal Voices 88

Trout In A Top Hat 59

Twirling 14

INDEX OF TITLES

Uncle Bernie's Beard 36

What Lies Beyond 49

When Forty Years Have Passed 122

Who Can Know 127

Witches 12

Zebra 10